Rin Asuka first Photobook

Location in Russia

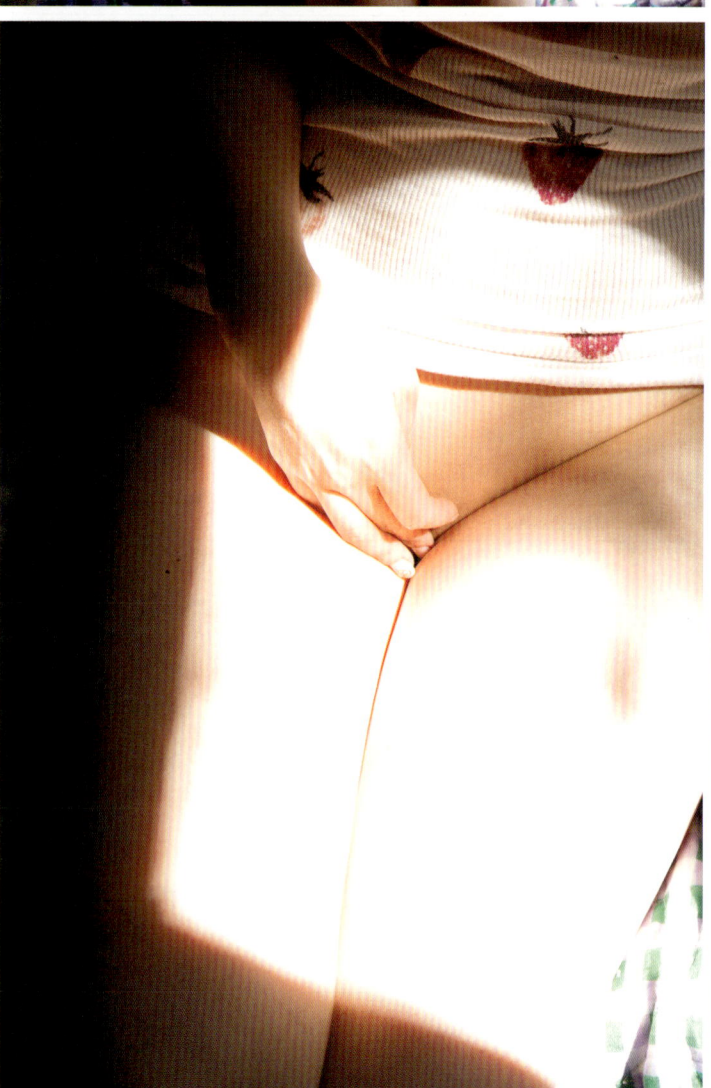

Rin Asuka first Photobook

Location in
Russia of Khabarovsk

Artist: RIN ASUKA
Photographer: SUSUMU MAKIHARA
Assistant Photographer: RINTARO URYU
Styling: MAI OOKA & RIN ASUKA
Hair and make-up: MAI OOKA
Artist Management: TADAHIKO GOTO
(EIGHTMAN PRODUCTION)

Art Director: RYOTA MIZUKI
Editor: HIROSHI SHIBATA (TAKESHOBO)

ありがと♡♡

A♡♡ ♡
♡♡ん♡

飛鳥りん